I Can Run

Murray Head

I Like to Read®

HOLIDAY HOUSE • NEW YORK

I Like to Read® books, created by award-winning picture book artists as well as talented newcomers, instill confidence and the joy of reading in new readers.

We want to hear every new reader say, "I like to read!"

Visit our website for flashcards and activities:
www.holidayhouse.com/I-Like-to-Read/
#ILTR
This book has been tested by an educational expert
and determined to be a guided reading level A.

Text copyright © 2017 by Parachute Publishing, LLC
Photographs copyright © 2012 by Murray Head
All Rights Reserved
HOLIDAY HOUSE is registered in the U.S. Patent and Trademark Office.
Printed and bound in May 2021 at Toppan Leefung,
DongGuan City, China.
www.holidayhouse.com
First Edition
3 5 7 9 10 8 6 4

Library of Congress Cataloging-in-Publication Data is available.

ISBN 978-0-8234-3831-0 (hardcover)
ISBN 978-0-8234-3846-4 (paperback)

For Brody, who I know can do
anything he decides to do.

I can run.

I can hop.

I can sit.

I can jump.

I can eat.

I can see.

I can run.

I can hide.

I can hide.

I can peek.

I Like to Read®

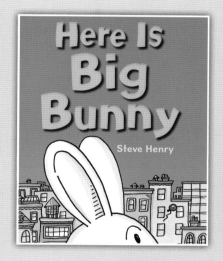

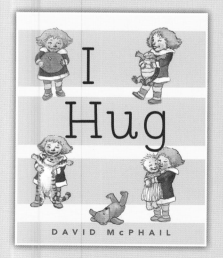

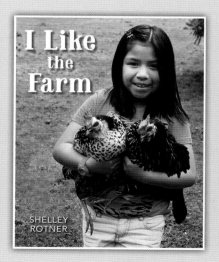